THE ANIMAL PSYCHOLOGIST

M. Foroozandeh

iUniverse LLC
Bloomington

THE ANIMAL PSYCHOLOGIST

iUniverse books may be ordered through booksellers or by contacting:

iUniverse
1663 Liberty Drive
Bloomington, IN 47403
www.iuniverse.com
1-800-Authors (1-800-288-4677)

ISBN: 978-1-4917-1726-4 (sc)
ISBN: 978-1-4917-1725-7 (e)

Library of Congress Control Number: 2014905632

Printed in the United States of America.

iUniverse rev. date: 05/22/2014

Preface

"Why did I write this?"

Why did I really write this? I don't know. I just know that I was thinking for some time that if I want to write a story this time, I will write something that differs with previous writings of mine and others. After reading it, readers can write about what they have perceived from this story. Whatever they have perceived, is what I have wanted to say and I've been able to. Or maybe I haven't been able to and made them perceive something that I hadn't intended. Perhaps the readers perceive something that has been in the hidden layers of my mind and I haven't been aware of it.

I would be very glad if readers email their opinions to me.

Mahmoodforoozandeh@yahoo.com

The judge, a plump man, and about fifty years old, comes angrily down the stairs and tells the interrogator, "I'll convict no other culprit until this roof is paved. This is the last time I mention this. My chair's hind legs are half sunk in clay. You call this a court?!" And leaves.

The interrogator, a forty-two years old man with black and disorderly beard, anxiously summons the accused through the servant. The interrogation session is held in the half-ruined justice hall, in one of the rooms still intact. A stout man, the interrogator sits at the desk. The accused, a man about thirty-two years old , enters and softly salutes. The interrogator mutters a reply to the thin man with the erect neck and says, "Sit down!" the interrogation starts.

The man sits across from him, setting his right arm, which i's plasters, on his lap.

"Some have seen you take the judge's car up on the roof of the house next to the court that is empty. What do you say?"

"Who has seen? Whoever has seen let him come testify before me."

"How did the car go up on the roof then?, On wings?"

"How do I know?"

"No one but you was against the judge. Say, why were you in jail in the first place?"

"For the toilet."

"How is that?"

"I was in the toilet, unaware that His Honor was waiting impatiently behind the door. As I came out, he shouted at me, 'What are you doing here in the justice hall toilet, you bum!'

I said, 'Bum is your father."

"Then he threw you in jail?"

"Of course."

"What happened then?"

"I wrote him from the jail and said sorry for cursing your father -- should've cursed all your ancestors."

"What did he do then?"

"Set me free."

"For what reason?"

"Said I was crazy."

"What did you say?"

"Said if I were crazy I would set your car on fire."

"And why didn't you?"

"Found no oil, search though I did."

"Was that before or after your jail?"

"After my jail."

"How long were you jailing?"

"Seven months."

"So they are right to say you took his car up on the roof?"

"They are not right, as I did no such thing."

"Four people have witnessed you, while you are only one. Assuming you are a fair witness in this affair, you are one against four witnesses. So obviously they are right. Besides, some have seen you look for oil."

"I told you –looked but didn't find. Besides, all by myself..."

"Maybe you had help."

"But you said those four saw me take the car myself..."

"Well, maybe those four didn't see your accomplice. Now that you're freed from jail after months, you're against the judge instead of thanking him?"

"But he ruined the justice hall."

"How does it concern you?"

"He did it on purpose so I couldn't use the toilet."

"There are so many departments, why should you use the justice hall toilet?"

"Nowhere is as good as the justice hall."

"Is the justice department for enforcing justice or not?"

"It is not for enforcing justice, but enforcing the law."

"What is the difference?"

"A lot! If they wanted to enforce justice, the judge was right— they had to demolish it."

"What is the source of your enmity with him?"

"Since when he was my teacher. One day a lady called him saying, "My child is too naughty at home." He said, "Should I punish him? No, replied the lady. 'Punish the child sitting next to him to scare him. 'Then he beat me as much as he could, although I didn't sit next to that child at all! But why?"

"The teacher was at fault. It is not fair. He should have been careful to punish the very next student. Not so with us in the justice department. We are at

pains not to breach any one's right. How old were you then?"

"Don't know."

"You look now about thirty or older."

"Older, older."

"The one who punished you wasn't the judge."

"He was too! He had a big soar on his cheek just like the judge."

"What job have you had meanwhile?"

"I was a teacher."

"What did you teach?"

"Animal psychology."

"Jailers have reported that you yelled at nights in your cell saying, "why did you create the world this way? '...What did you mean?"

"Because the world too is chaotic, like the justice department."

"I don't get it, do you agree or disagree with ruining the justice hall?"

"If it is to enact justice, I agree; but if it is to bar me from using the toilet, no way."

"By the way, the judge has never been a teacher, at least within the past years, because I have worked in the justice hall for the last 15 years and have always seen him here."

"So who punished me then?"

"How do I know?"

"Why do you say that if you don't know?"

"It must have been someone else."

"No one but him, like him had a sore on the cheek."

"His Honor has no sore."

"How come he has one when I look, and not when you do? Maybe that's like your four witnesses."

"You're not saying four fair witnesses have lied against you! Why should they?"

"How do I know?"

"Well now that's clear. Say why did you take the car up to the roof?"

"I hated the sight of his car."

"Why didn't you burn it like the previous judge's car?"

"I didn't burn that one's car. I have no wife."

"How does it relate to a wife?"

"Because to every woman who wanted divorce, he would issue a verdict on her behalf and grant her all the husband's assets."

"That wasn't the last judge, but the one before him, whose wife was kidnapped. So he had to leave her. Seems you know everything about the justice department."

You must've been after information. Whose informer have you been?"

"My mom's! Dozens refer to the justice dept. everyday..."

"But they are not spies. We checked them. They all pointed to you. And now you confessed."

"But my quarrel with the judge was only because I took too long and he was pissed off."

"Makes no difference. Why did you take too long in the toilet ? Maybe you were setting up wire tapping?"

"This tapping...what is it , in the first place?"

"Stop faking. All spies are that way. Well, tell me who else did you give the information to?"

"My aunt's!"

"What's her job?"

"She does people's laundry."

"So she gets information that way. Now, why did you fuss so in the prison yard?"

"Because they took me out of solitude."

"But weren't you worse off there?"

"Not at all, I sang and danced by myself. What better bliss than solitude in the world?"

"How...but books are full of complaints about loneliness."

"Nonsense. They don't understand."

"Well, say now , why did you cry blasphemies in your cell?"

"What blasphemy did I cry?"

"Do you know what blasphemy is? It means ingratitude toward God. So you've been a blasphemous spy who took the judge's car up on the roof...now I recall :maybe the woman we arrested for espionage was your aunt?"

"My aunt isn't into these stuffs .But I don't know why she's been arrested."

"When she was cooking and doing the laundry, she asked the judge's wife suspicions questions."

"What kinds of questions?"

"For example , she asked "why do you have too many children?""

"And her answer?"

"She said, 'None of your business, are you a maid or a spy?' I've read too many spy books. I know one of their ways is using laundresses... Now say about the hotel case! Your charges are not few.""

"That was nothing. We took an ass to the third floor to scorch. Some who had smelled kebob, ran upstairs. As the ass started to yowl, a hotel clerk nervously called the cops. Not my fault.""

"Whose idea was to scorch the ass?"

"The donkey him self."

"But why did you take him up to the fifth floor?"

"Not the fifth;, the third floor."

"Here it says the fifth floor."

"Wrong. Five star hotel, but third floor."

"But why did you take him to a hotel?"

"He didn't like other places."

"So why did he cry?"

"Because a hotel person took one of his carrots."

"So it wasn't because of scorching."

"Not at all. That's libel."

"How did the manager let you take him up?"

"I myself was the manager."

I've studied animal psychology."

"Well, did you pay him in return for scorching?"

"No, he said Just be a Good Samaritan."

"Such an ass."

"Ass is your dad."

"Be polite, you fool. This is a court."

"You are being offensive."

"I wonder how he let you scorch him without getting something from you!"

"Don't wonder. Not Everything is for money.

"Let's get to the point. How old is he?"

"Fifteen."

"How is his family life?"

"What's the point of these questions?"

"We want to make judgments based on psychological analysis so no one's rights are violated. You just answer!"

"He says he grew up with a step mother."

"Oh, poor thing."

"Why poor?"

"Because I myself grew up with a step mom."

"In fact he says she was kind. They are not like us."

"Didn't she pinch him on the sly?"

"Didn't say. But when his dad gave her kindly some oats, she went nuts .Once she burned the oats in the barn so he couldn't eat it."

"Just like my step mom."

"Your step - mom burned the oats too?"

"Worse. Anyway, how was he with his siblings?"

"What do you want with his siblings?"

"Well, you said you studied zoo psychology. We want to know what complex he had to want to be scorched. If he had any complex, we will lessen his punishment. That's justice for you. Where did you study?"

"Oxford."

"In Oxford you studied animal psychology?"

"No, I studied Russian literature there."

"But where did you study animal…"

"Cypress."

"How many brothers and sisters does he have?"

"Don't know exactly as his dad reproduced wherever he went. Said he had eight brothers & sisters from his own mom. But one brother is lame, because at his birth he was in a haste."

"Well, haste is waste. Anything else? By the way I heard you were a racing champion."

"Right. I ran a lot after bread."

"Did you get bread in the end?"

"No, but became a racing champ."

"Well, back to the main point. His familial relations must be investigated. Maybe he grew masochistic for their abuses. Can't just give a verdict."

"Who must investigate that?"

"Don't know that exactly. But we assigned similar cases to universities and research institutes. It's been reported that his dad was very proud of him …. Is he proud?"

"No, but he's pig-headed."

"What do you know about his mom?"

"Not much, except she gave birth two to three times a year and wouldn't relent."

"What do you know about his past?"

"I just know he was the lord's ass, but once the lord beat him badly and he went off to the wilderness."

"Why was he beaten, do you know?"

"He said once the lord's maids made him a tasty salty meal. Before serving it, the ass goes to the pot and eats from it. After the lord eats it all up, he noticed it was salty. Then he somehow finds out that the ass had eaten from it before him. So he gives orders to beat the beast for not telling him it was salty."

"Serves him right! And then?"

"Nothing. The beast ran off to freedom. In zoo psychology they say whatever throws you over , will enhance you."

"Well, what did he do now? Do you know?"

"He just made animals pregnant and ran off. I have heard"

"So that was his job. But didn't the lord send his servants after him?"

"Yes, but his job was now freedom. In zoo psychology they say the animal's character is formed by his job. Excuse me, I heard you arrested his dad?"

Searching through his papers the interrogator says casually, "That's right. One night in the street he was singing and disturbing the people's sleep."

"Did you find what he was singing?"

"Here, it was recorded, at midnight he was yelling:

Leave off cunning, o lover , go crazy , crazy

then come and leave out with the lovers.".

"Didn't he say why?"

With his head down the interrogator softly says, "He said he wanted to give the people food for thought…Tell me of his other traits."

"Another trait of these is that like us, they do not listen to advice. They must feel it."

"How is that?"

"Like when you tell them don't touch fire, they don't understand, but when they touch and burn, then they do."

"Strange! We don't have such issues in the field of law. Anyway, when he left the lord, what information about life did he have?"

"Like all freed prisoners, he knew nothing."

"How did he go to females then?"

"Maybe someone taught him. I just know they aren't decent, faithful and sincere like us. They go for anyone who comes across."

"Why do you think he doesn't surrender voluntarily?"

"He's scared of the lord's people."

"Why so?"

"They want to assassinate him. "

"Why?"

"Because he lived for a long time in the lord's house and knows the secrets of his life and wives. At psychoanalysis he kept saying, "Never again will I have salty food," and kept looking behind him."

"How did he meet you in the first place?"

"I told you, I am an animal psychologist."

"How did he know your address?"

"Come on, I'm the best animal psychologist in town. Not only they, but even humans know my address. One sunset, he came to my door and knocked. I said who's there?"

"He said, it's me."

"I opened the door, and asked him to come in."

"He said, wanted to commit suicide.

I knew at once he had depression."

"What did you do then?"

"I offered him to come in, insisted till he accepted. On the way, I noticed he was humming:

"Any prince or pauper who found a way to this tavern has nothing but his heart's blood in his goblet."

Then I was sure of my diagnosis. I psychoanalyzed him and prescribed medication. Two days later he came back and asked to be scorched."

"Didn't you advise him against it?"

"Not really. Well, I have to make a living too. Besides I thought scorching him will make him feel better and forget suicide. But he insisted it to be in a classy place and offered to pay whatever the cost."

"So you took him to the hotel."

"Not me. Gave him the hotel address. He came by taxi."

"Why didn't he refer to another psychologist?"

"Come on, who better than me?"

"But as reported, a physician was in touch with you too."

"Not a physician, but a dentist. For him we brought the dentist."

"What for?"

"He had a tooth-ache, but wouldn't go to the dentist."

"Who paid the wage?"

"Himself."

"Well, didn't you tell him the lord's assassins are after him?"

"He knew it."

"Tell me his other traits."

"Through his psychoanalysis I found he was raised motherless."

"Is she dead?"

"No, divorced."

"Why?"

"He said his dad used to count the fruits and put them in the fridge."

"Wasn't that out of caprice?"

"Don't suppose so."

"Well say, what does he like, what does he fear?"

"I don't know what he likes, besides carrots. Just know that when he curses anyone he says I hope your happy days are filled with toothache. So when he got a toothache he cried for a dentist, whereas when he had stomach ache he never cried for a belly doc."

"It's reported you took bribes from him to let him in to the hotel."

"He brought me some money , but no bribe."

"How much was it?"

"A lot, three to four big packets."

"And then?."

"I asked him, 'What do you bring this money as? If it is as a bribe I won't accept .But if you intend it as a gift, it's okay.' He said,'I swear it is only a gift.'"

"But were you the hotel owner to accept?

"No, but that concerned his intention, not the hotel owner's"

"Aren't you a teacher?"

"Yes, but afternoons I worked in a hotel."

"Didn't he say where he got the money? Not in a lottery!"

"I don't think so."

"Then?"

"I guess he pinched it from the lord and maybe that's why he insisted to be scorched --conscience pain."

"Maybe that why the lord's people are after him."

"Maybe."

"Well, why didn't he go back to give back the money and rid himself of the agony?"

"Because he needed it."

"Another question -what do you know about his ancestors?"

"I guess his ancestors too were donkeys."

"All right. Let's move on to other topics. What's their status in other regards, such as adultery?"

"As far as I know, there is no rape among them. Their females are quite bashful."

"How about incest?"

"That's totally taboo for them,"

"How about adultery?"

"I have no idea. If I say something, you demand evidence."

"In this particular case evidence is not mandatory!"

"Sorry I can't help you there."

"I think that's rare among them, as we have only two or three such files in the justice department. By the way, you said you studied in Oxford?"

"Russian literature."

"Does it relate to zoo psychology?"

"You know Russians have great respect for their animals?"

"You studied zoo psychology in the curriculum of Russian literature?"

"How can Russian go with zoo psychology?

"Well, say, do we have anything in common with them?"

"A lot. A lot."

"Such as?"

"Such as we don't like being scorched. Neither do they."

"What else?"

"When someone bothers them they kick them, and we undermine them. In other ways ,not much difference. Except we cover up everything, but they do not."

"How long do you think he will be on the run?"

"Till he can forfeit himself. According to zoo psychologists , he has fear of loss."

"Very interesting . We regard ourselves as entitled to others' services. How about them?"

"I don't suppose they are so."

"You mean they know better than expect from others?"

"In terms of reason, they are not better than us."

"Why do you think he doesn't give up running away?"

"I think he doesn't mean to ignore himself."

"Why?"

"When you wish to live free, then you can't ignore yourself."

"Why did he escape in the first place?"

"That day when people rushed upstairs…"

"Why?,why did people rush upstairs?"

"Because they had smelled kebob."

"Well!"

"Some hotel clerk who was himself a partner, got scared and called the cops. When the donkey saw the cop car from upstairs he cried in terror, I don't need so many enemies. Then he ran downstairs and away. The cops chased after him, but couldn't catch up."

"Where can he be now?"

"I don't know, but I remember at psychoanalysis he said, "When I was with the lord no one heard me." He may have gone where he will be heard."

"What did he mean by that?"

"In terms of animal psychology he meant he was seeking someone who is not self-infatuated, and lends an ear to his pains."

"Don't the self-infatuated hear the animals?"

"They hear no one."

"Go on – what other good traits do they have that we don't?"

"Their other good trait is they have no class."

"That's curious. Mankind has tried for thousands of years to make a classless society, but in vain."

"Still , they aren't far ahead of us."

"I wonder if there is love among them."

"What is love in the first place?"

"Love is the extravagant image one forms toward another being"

"And when the first beast sees he's been cheated he kicks in the other's rib. You call this love?"

"Be serious, this is a court of law."

"I am being serious .What should I say?"

"Another question .You better answer it right. What's their ideology ?"

"No ideology seemingly, but they seem to be for pleasure."

"Epicurean philosophy."

"I don't suppose he has heard Epicuruse's name, though in animal psychology that name is heard a lot."

"They don't need to hear it; it's enough to practice it."

"I don't think so, but tell me, is it good to have ideology?"

"Good if the idea is good, bad if not!"

"Some psychologists believe that ideology corrupts reason, but since they have no faith in anything, they don't lose their mind."

"Anything else you asked him at psychoanalysis?"

"I asked why were you born?"

"And his answer?"

"Said, I don't know."

"How is that possible?"

"Don't know, that was his answer any way."

"You should have pressed him to say."

"I pressed him a lot."

The interrogator mutters to himself, "I wish he had said, so we too would know why we came to this world."

"This time if I find him, I'll beat him so much to make him speak up. Once he said, "My mom kept giving birth to girls. My dad kept telling her to breed boys ,to no avail, then he beat her so much till she brought a boy."

The interrogator mutters, "I am of the same opinion, punishment should not be underestimated. We don't use the lash enough …But tell me, do they, like humans, justify things?"

"Unfortunately he said nothing in this regard."

"Do they have any leader?"

"How can animals have no leader? What are shepherds for?"

"I said leader, not boss…of their own kind."

"I see…in any heard a goat runs forth and others, sheep and donkeys, follow suit. In fact he said in the lord's stable there were seventy to eighty beasts and a goat who was the fore runner…"

"Was what?"

"Forerunner. You call them leader, we say footloose."

"Well?"

"Bothered them a lot."

"Like how?"

"He said he ate their oats slyly in the dark, kicked them and said, "Pardon me", and went to hiding."

"Well?"

"Anyhow, the beasts united after some consultation and elected a mule as leader .But the mule who used to talk of equality and fraternity, now makes their life so miserable that a part of them wanted to resort to that same goat."

"Didn't they tell the mule why he did so?"

"Yes, but he said, 'I am the leader, and am alone my judge, you have no right to ask me questions.'"

"Hadn't they clarified his leadership before electing him?"

"Yes, but he said, 'Nonsense- you just do your duties toward me.'"

"During the psychoanalysis didn't he say anything about his dad's temperament?"

"Yes, he said his dad was a pious man. Once he lost a fifty dollars bill he was going to buy oats with. Few days later by chance, he finds two fifty dollars bills...He takes one and puts the other where it was by a wall...because he said he lost only one bill and taking two would be impious."

"Is his dad obsessive?"

"No, but he washed his hands and face a lot ."

"That's it...These people, when they find any money, they leave half of it untouched.

More about his father!"

"Said his dad was so pious...never helped anyone for fear of God"

"I don't understand."

"Said God might think there's a trick up my sleeve and I'm helping the guy for my own sake."

"How so?"

"For ostentation and such."

"Strange!"

"Not strange .If God thinks so, he might lose the alms he has given away."

"Well, he could donate without ostentation."

"May be he doesn't mean to show off .But how can he know what God thinks?"

The interrogator puts his finger on his lips and says: "Wow! I hadn't thought about that .They're sometimes wiser than us. I, too, help others sometimes, I must be careful." To the man, he said, "I say, when the lord beat him, why didn't he file a complaint in the justice department? If he did maybe he wouldn't get depressed. How did he behave when he came to your house?"

"He was respectful, when we took him to brand him , he became very friendly...pity the cops came."

"Couldn't you get rid of them?"

"We would, but he ran away."

"Poor thing was scared of jail, but we are not as others think. Any one we put in jail, it is for

his own good."

"But you imprison even eighty years old men!.

"That's it...some have no proper food and accommodation. But how are they emotionally?"

"He is very emotional .When the doc wanted to pull out his tooth, he wept and cried, "What do wolves do in wilderness when they have toothache?"

"Tell me more about them ...I heard they use their urine organ for pleasure. True?"

"I don't know, how is that possible?"

"So you don't know. It's not right anyway. And about the lord, he didn't mean to beat him. Just wanted to cut his ear, but he refused. Then he was beaten.

Any way...it says here that you've badly beaten the local grocer?"

"It was his own fault. I owed him only 23 dollars, and every night he came to my dream. I pleaded with him to wait till I get my wage, but he wouldn't relent. One midnight I ran after him and I fell in a drainpipe. The lid had been stolen by junkies, but authorities pay no attention." He shows his arm cast in plaster.

"Must be careful when you run, especially at midnight.

Says here you have some writings,"

"I write merely about psychology .One must serve society through education as long as one lives."

"Right, go on!"

"I recently finished a text that publishers are fighting for."

"What is it about?"

"About how to make a friend out of a foe."

"Well, tell me a summary of it."

"In incidental encounters I look straight in my foe's eyes, grin and curse him. He sees my laughter, and my lips' movement, and happily comes to make up."

"So interesting!...Oh I was forgetting .Do they have mourning?"

"Yes , but he said it gets crowded only at dinner time."

"How about suicide?"

"They do that when they have no other plight. Do you think you can arrest him?"

"We already have. He and his dad will soon be tried."

The accused stares at him.

"Well, let's see the verdict: "For taking the judge's car up to the roof, blasphemy, spying, branding the ass in the fifth star hotel, and disturbing the peace, I convict you to fifteen years of public prison, without lashing."

The defendant rises and cries out :"No way! I hate public prison .I'd rather be jailed for 25 years but not in general prison,"

"Okay, since you're an educated guy, I do you this last favor: Fifteen years of solitary confinement."

Gaily laughing the defendant sits down:

"Oh, great .But Your Honor, are you the judge or prosecutor?"

"No difference. Whatever I say goes. The judge will not override me. Why? You're afraid he might change your sentence to the public jail? Rest assured. As I said fifteen years solitary cell."

The defendant rises, shakes hands with the interrogator , thanks him and goes to the door with the guard who hand cuffs him .

Before leaving the room, he asks: "Have you really seen the car on the roof-top sir?"

The interrogator says: "It's in the report,"and clears his file from the desk.

The song of the psychologist, heard from solitary confinement, made even the guardsmen who kept sentry, happy. His loveable loneliness, however, didn't last long. Four months later, the ceiling of his cell started dripping, and the floor was gradually getting watery. Reluctantly, he had to leave his cell and go to the public jail.

In the ward, among the ordinary prisoners, was a man who was called the "philosopher," apparently because he had been a university professor, teaching philosophy. His companion was known as the "writer," who was in prison because of his writings. After lunch, which consisted mostly watery beans or lentil stew, these two would sit beside the ward wall and would speak to the prisoners, who were sitting around them. And would answer their questions.

That day the philosopher was talking about "reality despotism." He said, "If the reality of society is mostly ignorance and idiotism, some corrupt tricksters or honest unwise people will hold its harness. Otherwise, if the reality of society is wisdom, it will naturally incline toward trustworthy and discerning people."

It had been almost three months since the animals escaped the Lord's stable. They were grazing when they colluded and ran away. A few weeks later, however, according to the law, they were with their own help captured.

Some of the animals, especially the sheep, also participated in the meetings of the philosopher and the writer, and tried to understand something of their talks. Four weeks into the psychologist's presence in the public prison, the interrogator sent for him. This time he was so kind. He ordered the servant to bring them tea and after some friendly conversation said to the psychologist:

"Since you're an educated man and I've been told that you attend the meetings of this philosopher and this writer, I want you to do something for me. A very simple job. "

"What job?"

"I want you to keep your friendship with them and inform us a little about their affairs."

"I'm not a rat."

"I don't want you to be a rat. Why do you interpret it like that? I'm just saying that when they go on leave, you do the same and see where they go. That's it."

"But then you may hurt them."

"No, no. We just want to know whom they speak with. There's nothing wrong with speaking."

"But if you want to hurt them, I don't accept."

"No, no. I swear on my child's life. Not at all."

"It's ok if it's going to be like that."

"By the way, a couple of days ago the prison clergyman, Haj Agha, came here and complained about you. And what a complaint!"

"I haven't done anything to him. He had a problem with Esmal Two-headed. It has nothing to do with me.

He defrauded him. I tried hard, but I couldn't get back his money."

"But he said that you mediated between them. Tell me the story from the beginning, so that I know exactly what happened."

"Esmal Two-headed told me, "You're an animal psychologist, and the clergyman respects you. Go invite him to give a homily for this friend of mine, who's been run over by a car. He was a decent man."

"And what did you do then?"

"I went to the second floor, to the prison's mosque, and invited Haj Agha. At first, he said that he was busy and didn't have time. I said, "Your compensation will be of course preserved." He said, "Please don't say that, it isn't worth that." And he accepted. Then he asked me, "What kind of person was he?" Said that he was known as a nice man. He came to Esmal Two-headed's home and started his homily. Esmal was sitting there and looking at the crowd and laughing in a certain way. Haj Agha complimented the decedent a lot and prayed to God to recompense and reward him. Four or five days later, I saw him in the prison yard. He came to me and after greeting bashfully brought up the matter of money. I thought Esmal Two-headed had given him it. As he told me that he had not, I immediately went to him, who was in the other ward. I asked him to pay Haj Agha as soon as possible. He repeated, "Sure, sure I will. I swear on your child who's dearer than my own, I'll give him his money by the day after tomorrow."

A few days later Haj Agha came to me in the yard again and said angrily "How can you be an animal psychologist and not know that this evil man won't ever pay me?" I was dumbfounded and speechless. He said, "This goddamned man held a mourning gathering for himself." Later, I heard from other prisoners that because he had committed too many crimes, he tried to pretend that he had a car accident and died. He has come here with a fake identity."

"Before Haj Agha, two of your neighbors had complained about you too. They said that in the middle of the night, some of the animals come behind your cell and caw and won't let them sleep."

"They came only one night, and since I wasn't aware they were there, they crowed to wake me. The same night, I assigned a code name for them, and since then whenever they'd come, one of them would sing the song I had taught them with a charming voice and I'd wake up."

"What was that code name or, according to the old-timers, watchword? "

"I had told them, "When you come, only one, not all of you, will sing 'Oh God, Rashti girl is pretty. Only that, so that I'd wake up."

"But how did they find you?"

"They sent a message to our donkey, saying, "We became homeless since the day we escaped. We couldn't even get enough fodder to eat. You tell us what to do." He replied, "I have no idea what you should do. I'm a foal myself and I don't know how to deal with my own affairs." He then told them to consult with me. He said, "He's an animal psychologist and can help you."

"They said in the interrogations that you guided them, so that they would get into prison and eat free food. That's why they came and gathered at the prison gate."

"It's never been like that. That's nonsense. I just said this place has good food. It's either lentil soup or beans, and they take no money for it, that's it. Weren't they under prosecution and weren't they supposed to get arrested? "

"They were under prosecution by law and for the Lord's complaint, but the cops couldn't find them in the desert until the day that they came to the prison gate and gathered there. The prison officers arrested them because they were unaware.

But you gave them the wrong advice. You increased our troubles. What they did themselves was the best thing. They escaped and we chased them. "

"I didn't tell them to come so that they arrest you."

"The government won't increase the prison budget, yet they expect us to arrest whomever they want right away and put them in jail."

He said softly, as if speaking to himself:

"All of the problems refer to lawlessness. If we make the prisoners spend for expenses, they wouldn't think of getting into prison for free dinner and lunch."

And he told the psychologist: "Well, we'll take care of their complaint later."

The psychologist wondered: "Look who's threatening me." The interrogator continued:

"Tomorrow, the writer is going on a leave. I'll tell the warden to give you a leave too. I want you to do your job seriously. Do you want more tea?"

The psychologist stood up and returned to the prison. Two days later he went to the court again and gave his report to the interrogator:

"I followed him yesterday, sir."

"Well?"

"He went and ate a baklava, bought a belt, then went to a newsstand, gave the newspapers a look, and picked up a few newspapers and magazines."

"Well, he didn't see anybody?"

"Yeah, I'd say. He went to a bookstore. I went to the snack bar across the street. He greeted someone, put his face near this person's ear, and said, "We need somehow to overthrow the regime.""

"Well done, but be careful. We are proud to have people like you. What happened next? "

"He went to a restaurant. I stood behind the wall of an alley in front of it and waited for him. Stood there a long time, but he didn't come out. Then I realized the restaurant had another door and he went out from that door."

"Why didn't you go looking for him in the restaurant?"

"Had already eaten lunch."

"That would have been fine, eat lunch again."

"But that would be squandering."

"Was it because you had no money?"

"Had a little money, but I needed it."

"Anyway don't worry about that. If you have to eat lunch, we had it budgeted this year and next year after Parliament approval, would have paid you the money."

"And if Parliament doesn't approve?"

"We've thought about that, too. Next year will budget it again and take it to Parliament. I told you not to worry about it. That's it, now tell me what the prisoners do there."

"They try to make life easier by mocking each other, which often leads to a brutal fight between them."

"What about the animals?"

"Their situation is not bad, but since they brought this female donkey, the situation has become a bit cluttered. Why have they arrested her?"

"She swaggered in the street."

"It wasn't for improper veiling?"

"No, I don't think so."

"But recently they also brought another donkey."

"That would be her nephew."

"But I saw that they sometimes have sex with each other."

"I don't think so. How is it possible? With his own aunt!?"

"Why did you arrest him?"

"He was carrying drugs."

"And what about the owner?"

"The drugs were found in his saddle bag. Shall we arrest the owner?

What do the other animals do?"

"Nothing. All of them are quiet, only sometimes I see our male donkey annoying the female donkey. A few days ago, when she was rolling on the cement of the prison yard and sunbathing, all the prisoners were standing and looking at her envyingly, but no one bothered her. When she stood up and started to walk in the yard strutting, suddenly our male donkey began singing."

"And what did he sing?"

"He sang "If lovers ravish the heart like this, they will penetrate preachers' faith."

This morning, before I wanted to come here, I saw that the prison yard was suddenly crowded. When I went further, saw that the female donkey was saying angrily, "I am born to enjoy my life but this donkey doesn't let me."

"And what did he say?"

He said, "I don't say anything, I just say let's do it together."

"And then?"

"Then she said, "Ay, I'm not that miserable to have sex with a beggar like you."

He said, "If she makes it with me, I will do everything she wishes. Even if she tells me to take possession of Russia, I'll go and do it."

"What happened next?"

"Then her nephew put his chest forward and said to the male donkey, "Leave my aunt alone, otherwise you will be in trouble!" At that moment his father came with his great black physique and slapped the son on the face and said, "Get lost, idiot. Aren't you ashamed of yourself, bothering this lady?" And said to the others, "This bastard doesn't do anything right." Then went towards the female donkey, bowed and kissed her hand and said, "Forgive him please with your generosity, this kid is foolish." She replied, "I'll forgive him for you, but this is the last time. They are really correct when say, 'Be a donkey, but don't get involved with a donkey.'" Then she went to the other side of the yard and stood in a corner."

"And then?"

"Nothing. A few minutes later, the father donkey bent his head and went toward her slowly and stood next to her. I don't know what he said to her ear that she immediately became short and they copulated. But then suddenly the donkey fell down and collapsed. We ran to see what had happened. Whatever cold water they poured on his face and sugar water that they gave him, he didn't awake. His son said, "A few months ago he sold his kidney and bought hay. Probably it's because of that." One of the prisoners kicked his stomach hard and said "Idiot donkey, you are sick unless you have to be." He suddenly shook, stood up, and said, "Who the fuck was that? Whoever he is, that donkey is his own father."

"You said that he mated with that female donkey in public?"

"Yes, sir."

"And the prison officers didn't do anything?"

"They didn't, sir. They watched and envied him."

"And Warden?"

"He said, "Unfortunately, we cannot do anything in this case. We have no law."

"It is also true, all of the problems are due to lawlessness."

"Can't you enact a law?"

"Yes, we will think about it. Parliament must approve it. Let's go to the other issues. What do the sheep do there? "

"They are obedient. They believe in the things that they don't know and adhere to them strictly."

"And the mule?"

"He is very stubborn. He always wants to go through the wall with his head."

"Didn't you tell him that doing this needs spade and pick?"

"Yes, but he says, "I am a leader. I know things you don't.""

"Does anybody admit that he is a leader?"

"He admits it himself and says, "I am a leader until the end of my life.""

"Sooo!"

After a short pause the interrogator said, "By the way, I remember something. Didn't you say that your family were villagers? But how did you end up in England?"

"That's a long story. It was all because my father set the king's crown on fire."

"The king's crown? What does that have to do with it? How could your father take the king's crown?"

"Through the Eshno cigarette."

"I don't get it!"

"At that time, we were living in a black tent. There was a gendarme whose post of duty was nearby. Once every few days he came to our tent with his bike and my dad received him with everything we had. Before he left, my father would give him some meat, yoghurt, or something else. One day he came and said "I haven't been paid for five months", and whined a lot. That day, we didn't have anything to give him. Two or three days later he came again and spoke about his problems once more. We made some tea for him. My dad offered him a cigarette and put a cigarette between his lips and lit it. Here, the gendarme suddenly jumped up and said, "No, no, there's no way, I can't let go of it. I respect our friendship, but reverence for the crown is something else." My father, who was amazed, asked, "What happened?" He replied, "Don't you know?! Get up, get up! It is a matter of national dignity, you can't joke with that." My dad asked again and again, "What happened?" he said, "You'll know that when we go to the police station. You set the king's crown on fire and ask what happened?" He pointed to his cigarette. My dad understood what was going on. He had lit the cigarette from the crown side. He begged and pleaded, but the gendarme would not relent. My dad finally realized that he wanted money. So he put his hand under the felt and picked up some money, that he hides there for a rainy day and brought it and put it in his pocket to apologize. The gendarme said, "I swear on our friendship, if you were anyone else it would have been impossible for me to let you to go."

"Well, what's the connection with your going to England?"

"Don't rush me please. We didn't have meat to give him every day. It is customary between the pastoralists, when a goat, sheep, or something else falls off the hill or mountain, to take its head off and, so it does not rot, divide it among the neighbors.

One day we had a case like that when the gendarme showed up. He said, "You're lucky that you don't need to buy meat. It costs a bomb! My children haven't eaten meat for six months."

I guess he went up the hill and sneakingly threw down a sheep or a goat that had lagged behind the flock, because he had been seen thereabouts a few times. Anyway, my father couldn't stand that. The gendarme had picked up a bad habit and we couldn't cope with him. So he sold the sheep flock and with the money bought a huge old house in the city and became a janitor in a company. A few years later, a boulevard was built near the house and its price rose much."

"And your father sold the house and gave the money to you to go abroad and study?"

"Bravo! That's how I went to England and the rest is history."

"I see. By the way, and before I forget, how were the English girls? I got a grant. I'm going to go there too to study."

"Very good. They were exquisite."

"I mean were they chaste?"

"They're very very chaste. The English girls are famous for being chaste."

"And the Cypriot girls?"

"They are too. God bless them."

"Now let's get to the heart of the matter. I've been told that when the philosopher goes on leave, he first takes a walk in the town to lose track and then goes to the Great fruit market. He has done that a few times so far..."

"Great fruit market? Perhaps because they bring fruits from all cities."

"Well, yes, trucks come from different cities and probably some people come there with them, and the philosopher goes there to make some arrangements with them. I want to know what they are plotting. Your mission is to discover their plot by every means."

"But in general, he's not a bad guy."

"You do your duty. I hear he had a fight with the mule?"

"The mule had a fight with him."

"What was the matter?"

"A few days ago, when he came to the yard to go to the prison office, the sheep gathered around him and told him, "You tell us what to do. The goat turned out to be like that, and the mule too. So who do we select as our leader to guide us?" He said, "Nobody! As long as you are looking for a leader, you won't ever be saved. You should try to become a rhino. There's no other way." One of the sheep asked "But what do rhinos do?" He answered, "The rhino travels alone." They asked, "What does that have to do with it?" The philosopher said "A lot. You think about that. Tell me your thoughts when I come back from the prison office."

"And?"

"When he came back, the sheep gathered around him again and said, "We thought a lot, but found no answer, except that the rhino has a horn on his nose." The philosopher said "You don't need that horn much. The only thing you need is to know that you don't need a leader." One of the sheep said, "He's right. If the rhino had a leader, he would wait to see where his leader would take him and he followed him. And he may fall in a well or fall down a hill, but when he travels alone, he decides for himself." One of the sheep said, "But then he may fall in the well too." The philosopher answered him "It is better for a being to become the victim of his own mistake, rather than someone else's mistake."

"And then?"

"Then the philosopher said, "This is the main principle of this matter. The rhino is his own leader. He travels hundreds of kilometers alone." And then when he wanted to go to his ward, the mule that had hid behind the kitchen wall and had listened to him ran after him and kicked his butt hard and said:

"You son of a bitch, you provoke them against me. Stupid man, don't you understand that the leader never makes a mistake? You deserve being in jail. You can't correct yourself."

"Well done! He did well.

But I've heard that the sheep have run away."

"They've probably gone to become rhinos."

"But wait. How could they run away? The ward's report about this hadn't been given to me yet."

"The warden told me that some of them frequently came to him and complained that they came from the desert and had become depressed at the prison. They begged him to open the big gate, so that they could see outside. They ran away as soon as he opened the gate."

"So the sheep fooled him?"

"Oh yeah. When I asked him why, he sighed and said, "Since I'm myself a nice guy, I think others are like me."

"That's it. I knew this so-called philosopher is only a conspirator. Why do I say that he needs to be watched? In college he said to his students that if you want to destroy an ideology, help it to gain power. They've gone on to become rhinos so that, as he says, they won't need a leader, though even humans can't live without a leader.

He had said that, an ideology must be unreachable if it wants to be sensational. But we are the only country in the world, whose beggars go to work by taxi.

I don't know if you've read the book "Waiting for Leader".

"No."

"The writer of this book shows with undeniable proof that not only the living, but also the dead need a leader."

"Why? Did he explain why?"

"Yes, but unfortunately, I haven't read the book yet."

After he drank his tea, and leaned against the chair to rest a bit, asking, "By the way, what did you do in your cell? Did you think about your wife and child?"

"No, I don't have a wife. I divorced her."

"Why?"

"She was always nagging. Repeatedly said that she wished had married her previous suitor. I told her that he was more junk than me, but she wouldn't accept that."

"Didn't you marry again?"

"No."

"Do you have a reason?"

"I like women who use their mouths just for eating and saying."

"And saying good words, of course."

"Exactly."

"Say, what then did you do in that cell alone?"

"I thought."

"About what? About your life?"

"No. I never think about myself. I think about human destiny. We had a tenant, who yelled at his son when he got mad at him and said, "Damn you. You wouldn't have been born if the condom hadn't been torn. You don't deserve living this life." In my cell, I thought how many thousands or tens of thousands of people have been born that way."

"It's interesting. I hadn't thought about it before. I remember that some time ago, I read in the papers that even one these people became the president of a country."

"Now you think what happens when the destiny of the mankind falls into the hands of people like him."

"I agree that rubbers play an important role in our lives today. There are lots of people who come to this world or leave it because of the bursting of these rubbers. By the way, I wanted to ask you a few times, but I forget. How did you come to have this scar on your forehead? It's almost new."

"Since the day I had an argument with the judge in the rest room. When he started shouting, the guards came in and knocked my head into the wall."

"Now I understand why the judge freed you so soon! Ok, let's do our own business. Where were we?"

"With the philosopher."

"Oh yes, I remember. I'll tell the warden to accept his request immediately, whenever he wants a leave, and to let you know too. Follow him and find out where he goes. As I said before, he frequently goes to the Great fruit market. Go there to find out whom he contacts."

And after a short pause, which was due to his writing, he continued, "By the way, I told the judge that you're cooperating with us. You're not offended by him anymore, right?"

"Of course, I am. The problem is not just this."

"What else is it? He has probably told you something in class?!"

"Yes. It's all about those days. Once he was advising us in class to be always honest, even if we sustain a loss. Then he went to this topic to ask the kids what job they wished to have in the future. Every one of them stood up and said something. One said that he wished to become a doctor, one said an engineer, and one said a pilot. When he asked me, I said that I wanted to become a knife stabber, so that everybody would be afraid of me, like black Hosein. He told me "Sit down, you silly. What kind of job is that?!" And when I talked back, he told me: "Get out of here, you asshole." In the end, he said that he wouldn't let me into the class unless I bring my father to school. The day after that, I took my father to him. My dad begged him to forgive me since I was just a kid and foolish. The judge said, "This kid talks nonsense." I said, "Didn't you say that we must tell the truth even if we sustain a loss?" He said, "Shut up you idiot. It has nothing to do with that." Eventually, after my father begged him a lot, he let me go back to my seat."

"Didn't your father punish you then?"

"No, I gave him a copper pot and he went away."

"I don't get it."

"He wasn't my father. He was a second-hand dealer. We had a lot of copper pots."

"I see."

He smiled.

"Now you may go back or do whatever you want to until next time."

He arose and, because he could not tolerate being away from the prison, went back there right away.

A few days later, the psychologist, the philosopher, and the writer were standing in the prison yard and making jokes. The psychologist told the philosopher, "The previous time, I brought him to his knees. Tomorrow is your turn."

The writer asked, "What did you tell him about me?"

The psychologist replied, "I told him that you and your friend were going to overthrow the regime." Everybody laughed loudly, and the philosopher told him, "When you're chasing me, be careful not to be run over by cars, because you are absent-minded." And again, the sound of their laughter rose. The warden, who was watching them through the window of his room, told himself, "He has penetrated them well. Bravo!"

After the psychologist left, the philosopher told the writer, "Poor man, since they've knocked his head to the wall, he's become absent-minded."

"Reason?"

"He had an argument with the judge. The guards attacked him. He was in a coma for one month. He was imprisoned once and was released. Now, they have brought him here again."

Two days later, around noon, he arrived at the run-down justice department. Before the interrogator asked him, he started with excitement, giving his report.

"Sir, I followed him."

"And?"

"He went to a lot of places, but he didn't contact anybody. Then I saw that he took a taxi. I took a taxi too right away."

"And?"

"He got out of the taxi near the Great fruit market. Then went among the trucks and started to check their plate numbers."

"I knew that! What else?"

"He checked a lot of truck numbers until he reached an eighteen-wheeler that was filled with watermelons."

"And? "

"When he bent over to read the plate number, another truck, a ten-wheeler, reversed and hit him hard."

"Well?! "

"People gathered, there was a big fuss. Then some guys took a taxi, put him into it and took him to the hospital. I immediately took a taxi too and chased him."

"Well?! "

"They drove him there and he was hospitalized."

"Do you know if he's alive?"

"I don't think he's dead, because one of the men I had seen before, said that he was still breathing."

"Well done! Little by little you're becoming a pro. Those who took him to the hospital may have conspired with him.

We must be after it. You must go to the hospital to check on him again."

"Sure, sir, but I paid five dollars for taxi."

"It's ok. I'll tell them to budget it and give it to you next year. Would you like a cup of tea?

The psychologist stood up, thanked him for the taxi fare, and returned to the Jail. In the ward, he told the prisoners the story of the philosopher's accident in the Great fruit market and it caused them grief. The writer said, "Once I told him to be careful about trucks, when you go to the fruit market. They don't know the difference between city and desert. But it turns out that he had turned a deaf ear to me."

The psychologist said, "Apparently you know about his life more than we do.

Why did he go to the Great fruit market a lot? Did he have an appointment with someone there?" The author said, "No, what appointment?! During his youth he was in love with a girl from Shiraz town. For this reason, he likes the cars with Shiraz town plate numbers. He went among the trucks and found them."

The next day, in the afternoon, when it was the appointment time, the psychologist went to the hospital. The philosopher didn't have anyone visit him. He was lying on the bed and whined with closed eyes."

The psychologist kissed his forehead and placed an ear near the philosopher's mouth, because he thought that the philosopher might have a request.

He listened carefully and understood that he was saying, "Damn on the all of trucks from Shiraz!" Now the working hours were over and the interrogator was gone. The next morning he went to the court and gave his report to him.

"Sir, I went to the hospital."

"And did you see him?"

"Yeah, I saw him."

"He was alive, right?"

"Yeah, but he is pretty bad. He's whining all the time."

"So,the result?"

He told of the philosopher's love during his youth for the interrogator and said what he heard when he put his head close to the philosopher's mouth. The interrogator paused for a while and then said, "I said the very first day that it is impossible that there's a conspiracy. The conspiracy and the fruit market!? What's the connection? Do you drink tea? Shall I tell them to bring some for us?"

After a little discussion of any topic, the interrogator once again asked about the sheep. The psychologist replied, "I said, they have gone to become rhinos." He asked the interrogator to order to have his cell roof fixed as soon as possible, because he was uncomfortable in the public jail. The interrogator said, "Since you've done your duty well, I will order it done today."

"Is the judge's car still on the roof?"

"It was apparently a misunderstanding. There was no car on the roof."

He continued:

"The judge is very happy these days. Each defendant they bring him is immediately accused by him, because they paved his building roof."

And then he said:

"A few days ago I talked with him about you. After much persistence, he finally said, "If he promises that he's no more going to the justice for toilet, I am ready to release him."

"I won't promise any such thing."

And he got up to go back to prison. Before going he said, "Wait, this prison is too large, specifically its yard. The animals are too relaxed and free. There was once a…"

The interrogator interrupted him, "Previously there was a university. Don't you want to drink tea again?"

A few days later they repaired the roof of his cell and he returned to his lovely solitary jail, where the guards once again enjoyed his singing.